The Sun
Is So Quiet

The Sun Is So Quiet

DISCARD

Poems by Nikki Giovanni

Illustrations by Ashley Bryan

Henry Holt and Company • New York

To
Connie Harris
—N.G. and A.B.

Contents

Winter

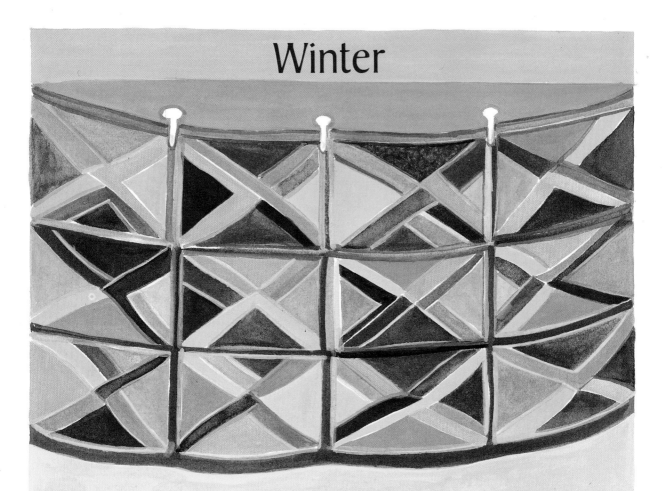

Frogs burrow in the mud
snails bury themselves
and I air my quilts
preparing for the cold

Dogs grow more hair
mothers make oatmeal
and little boys and girls
take Father John's Medicine

Bears store fat
chipmunks gather nuts
and I collect books
for the coming winter

Covers

Glass covers windows
to keep the cold away

Clouds cover the sky
to make a rainy day

Nighttime covers
    all the things that creep

Blankets cover me
    when I'm asleep

Snowflakes

Little   boys   are   like
Snowflakes
No   two   are   alike

Missing   teeth   skinned   elbows
            Always
Stinky   sticky   slippery
            Sweaty   and   Sweet

November

snowflakes waltz around my ears
i twirl in rhythm to the dance
of peppermint dreams
and mistletoe

kissing you

snowflakes ballet in my heart
warming me to crystal dreams
of dancing to that midnight sun

kissing you

snowflakes laugh and go away
taking dance and crystal dreams
leaving me   alone with you
to falalalalalalalala

Prickled Pickles Don't Smile

Never tickle
a prickled pickle
'cause prickled pickles
Don't smile

Never goad
a loaded toad
when he has to walk
a whole mile

Froggies go courting
with weather reporting
that indicates
There are no snows

But always remember
the month of December
is very hard on your nose

Winter Poem

once a snowflake fell
on my brow and i loved
it so much and i kissed
it and it was happy and called its cousins
and brothers and a web
of snow engulfed me then
i reached to love them all
and i squeezed them and they became
a spring rain and i stood perfectly
still and was a flower

Rainbows

If I could climb
    the mountains
And rest on clouds
    that float
I'd swim across
    the clear blue air
To reach my rainbow boat

My rainbow boat
    is oh so big
And I could be
    so tall
As I sit
    in my captain's chair
The master of it all

But I am just a little boy
    who's standing on the ground
And others steer
    the rainbow past
While I just hang around

I sit on the ground
    and see
The rainbows steering
    right past me
I sit on the ground
And wonder *why*

Kisses

Flowers for hours
remain inert
but when the bees pass
they flutter and flirt

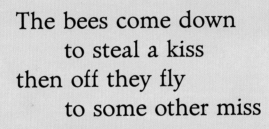

The bees come down
   to steal a kiss
then off they fly
   to some other miss

Strawberry Patches

Through the green clover and white-tipped violets
and brown-flecked bunnies and laughing pin-striped
chipmunks

(Being very careful
of the dandelions shedding
their yellow spring coats)

Little girls   tip toe   into the meadows
playing hide
and seek

in the strawberry patch

The Reason I Like Chocolate

The reason I like chocolate
is I can lick my fingers
and nobody tells me I'm not polite

I especially like scary movies
'cause I can snuggle with my mommy
or my big sister and they don't laugh

I like to cry sometimes 'cause
everybody says, "What's the matter
don't cry"

and I like books
for all those reasons
but mostly 'cause they just make me
happy

and I really like
to be happy

The Stars

Across the dark and quiet sky
When sunbeams have to go to bed
The stars peep out and sparkle up
Occasionally they fall

They dance the ballet of the night
They pirouette and boogie down
In blue and red and blue-white dress
They hustle through the night

The fairies play among the stars
They ride on carpets of gold dust
And Dawn's gray fingers shake them off
Occasionally they fall

Racing Against the Sun

I ride the rainbow . . . spinning around
blending . . . bending . . . down through the stars
winding my way . . . to the ocean of Dreams
       Racing against the sun

There isn't much time . . . I have so much to do
I forge westward Ho with a dream or two
for all the boys and girls warm in their beds
       Waiting for the sun

I'm like the wind . . . I can't be seen
Whispering through . . . on the dust of moonbeams
I blanket the world . . . with peppermint dreams
       Home before the sun

Connie

quiet . . . like the sound of a cumulus cloud floating
by . . . or a butterfly fluttering its wings . . . no
sound . . . just a casual patience . . . a waiting for the pie
to come from the oven . . . the cream to peak at its
whipping . . . the idea that will make it all right

quiet . . . like a blue sky on a summer day . . . no rain
coming . . . but no drought worries . . . just walk in the
grass days . . . barefooting life . . . eluding
chiggers . . . cheating something . . . but not ourselves

quiet . . . like a quilt on a feather bed . . . and frost on
the window . . . we write our names knowing . . . the sun
will melt them off

but the sun is so quiet . . . that we don't care

we smile

Henry Holt and Company, Inc.
Publishers since 1866
115 West 18th Street
New York, New York 10011

Henry Holt is a registered trademark
of Henry Holt and Company, Inc.

Published in Canada by Fitzhenry & Whiteside Ltd.,
195 Allstate Parkway, Markham, Ontario L3R 4T8.

Library of Congress Cataloging-in-Publication Data
Giovanni, Nikki.
The sun is so quiet: poems / by Nikki Giovanni; illustrations by Ashley Bryan.
Summary: A collection of poems primarily about nature and
the seasons but also concerned with chocolate and scary movies.
1. Children's poetry, American. [1. Nature—Poetry. 2. Seasons—Poetry.
3. American poetry.] I. Bryan, Ashley, ill. II. Title.
PS3557.I55S86 1996 811'.54—dc20 95-39357

ISBN 0-8050-4119-2
First Edition—1996
Printed in the United States of America on acid-free paper.∞
1 3 5 7 9 10 8 6 4 2

The artist used gouache and tempera paint on Fabriano 100/100
cotton paper to create the illustrations for this book.

Permission for use of the following is gratefully acknowledged:
Lawrence Hill Books for "November" and "Racing Against the Sun"
© 1973, 1993 by Nikki Giovanni.
William Morrow and Company, Inc., for "Winter," "Covers," "Snowflakes,"
"Prickled Pickles Don't Smile," "Winter Poem," "Rainbows," "Kisses,"
"Strawberry Patches," "The Reason I Like Chocolate," and "The Stars"
© 1972, 1978, 1980 by Nikki Giovanni.

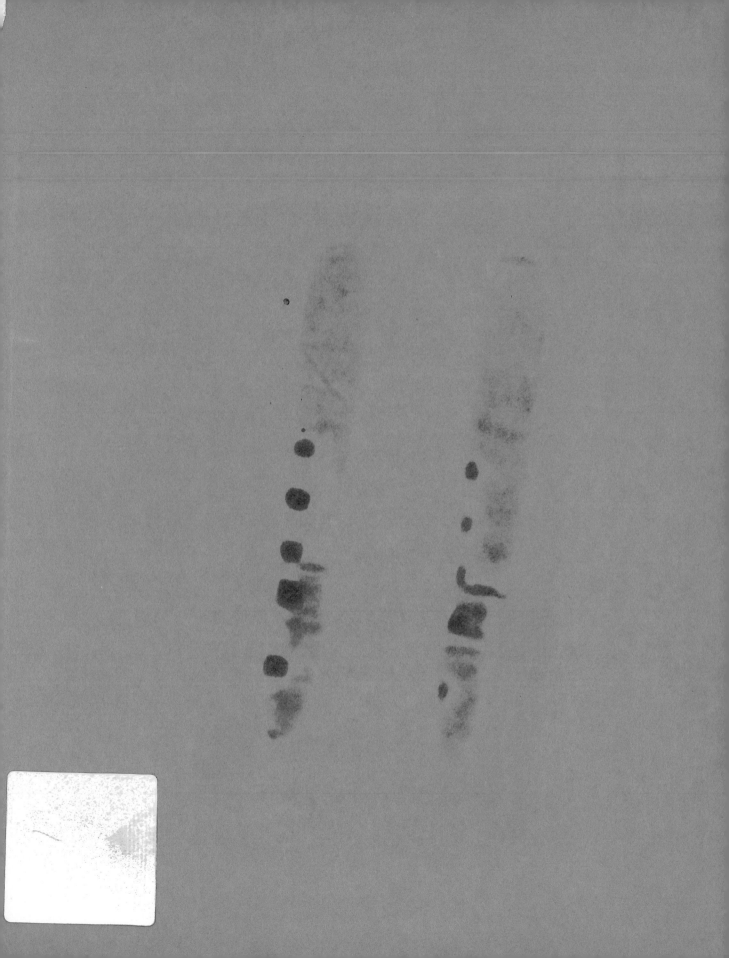